this is me

my best friend

Cheyenne Warwick

Lotta Petermann

little sister of

Chanelle Warwick

my mom

Sabrina Petermann

loves to shop online

Member of our gang

Paul Kennedy

WK

Robert Petermann

teacher

HANNIBAL

MY LIFE AS LOTTA

How Lamb is That?

Alice Pantermüller
Daniela Kohl

STERLING CHILDREN'S BOOKS
New York

An Imprint of Sterling Publishing Co., Inc.
1166 Avenue of the Americas
New York, NY 10036

Originally published as "Mein Lotta-Leben. Wie belämmert ist das denn?" by Arena Verlag GmbH written by Alice Pantermüller and illustrated by Daniela Kohl

ISBN 978-1-4549-3625-1

Library of Congress Cataloging-in-Publication Data

Names: Pantermüller, Alice, author. I Kohl, Daniela, 1972- illustrator.
Title: How lamb is that? / Alice Pantermüller ; illustrated by Daniela Kohl.
Other titles: Wie Belämmert ist das denn? English
Description: New York : Sterling Children's Books, [2019] I Series: My life as Lotta ; book 2 I Originally published in German: Wurzburg, Germany : Arena Verlag, 2012 under the title, Wie belämmert ist das denn? I Audience: Grades 4-6. I Summary: "Now that Lotta is settling into middle school, her life appears to be calming down...somewhat. So she has more time to focus on the really important stuff like more outrageous, everyday adventures with Cheyenne!"-- Provided by publisher.
Identifiers: LCCN 2019031109 I ISBN 9781454936251 (hardcover)
Subjects: CYAC: Best friends--Fiction. I Friendship--Fiction. I Family life--Fiction. I Middle schools--Fiction. I Schools--Fiction. I Humorous stories.
Classification: LCC PZ7.1.P35748 How 2019 I DDC [Fic]--dc23
LC record available at https://lccn.loc.gov/2019031109

Distributed in Canada by Sterling Publishing Co., Inc.
c/o Canadian Manda Group, 664 Annette Street
Toronto, Ontario M6S 2C8, Canada
Distributed in the United Kingdom by GMC Distribution Services
Castle Place, 166 High Street, Lewes, East Sussex BN7 1XU, England
Distributed in Australia by NewSouth Books
University of New South Wales, Sydney, NSW 2052, Australia

For information about custom editions, special sales, and premium and corporate purchases, please contact Sterling Special Sales at 800-805-5489 or specialsales@sterlingpublishing.com.

Manufactured in Canada

Lot #:
2 4 6 8 10 9 7 5 3 1

09/19

sterlingpublishing.com

Alice Pantermüller

MY LIFE AS LOTTA

How Lamb is That?

Illustrated by Daniela Kohl

For Andreas, my most loyal fan
and patient funny-face model.

 Daniela

TUESDAY, SEPTEMBER 6

Today I woke up
to this **squawking.**

It sounded like
a chainsaw.

SQUAWK!

But this is normal,
now that I'm
looking after **Hannibal.**

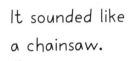

Hannibal is our neighbor
Mrs. Lopez's parrot. ⇨
She's in the hospital.

And because until recently, I wanted my own
animal 🐑 🐰 🐕 🐈 like crazy, now I've got
Hannibal.

For at least **three weeks.**
That's still nineteen days,
because so far it's only been two.

SQUAWK!

5

Parrots are actually nice, but unfortunately, Hannibal is a cockatiel, which Mom once told me is also called Nymphicus hollandicus. And I think the **nymphs** make him sick. He must be in a lot of **pain,** the way he squawks. Plus he bites. 🙁

Parrot

Nice Bird + Nymphs - Cockatiel

Now that Hannibal's around, suddenly I love going to school.

Since summer vacation ended, I've been in class 5b at ⟨ Wilt Whatman Middle School ⟩.

Which is great, because my very, very best friend Cheyenne is also in 5b.

the very best Cheyenne

What isn't so great is that Bernadette Bester is also in 5b. Because **Bernadette**→ thinks that she's **way better** than everyone else. But actually, she's

Bernadork Bester
← haha

1. totally stuck up with **her stuck-up nose** ─────→

2. and her **long blonde hair** ------

3. and her **rich parents**

4. and her own **horse**

Secret

5. and her **Girl squad,** with almost **all** the girls ── in our grade, except a couple. Like Cheyenne and me.

Emma, Maggie, Hannah

6. Plus she has the **coolest brother** in school.

Kevin

7. Which is why most girls in our class think she's **Great.**

WRONG
Bernadette is great

8. All **except Cheyenne and me!!!**

Before math class today, Bernadette passed out invitations to her birthday. "Wanna bet we don't get one," Cheyenne hissed. She was ready to stick her gum in Bernadette's math book.

But then we both got one! Because Bernadette was throwing a **HUGE OVERNIGHT CAMPING PARTY** and inviting **everyone** from our class. Even the boys.

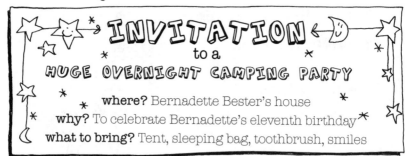

What a showoff, I'm just saying.

But Cheyenne and I were still psyched, especially because now we could plan a **funny** present for Bernadette. We spent all of math class brainstorming and passing notes.

hehehe

→ Cheyenne

We were giggling a lot, which Mrs. Crabbert didn't exactly love. Mrs. Crabbert is our teacher. And she's pretty **strict.**

I had just written down an extra nice gift idea, when she swooped in and took the note.

yikes!

And read it. And then gave us a weird look. →

???

Booger-flavored lip gloss?

We nodded. That's when she gave us an extra assignment as **punishment.** ☹

> She's just jealous because she wants booger-flavored lip gloss.

Which made me giggle again. 😊

For the rest of math class, we couldn't stop giggling. Our **ideas for Bernadette** were just so funny:

🎁 **Hannibal** with a pink ribbon around his neck. Or—better yet—his beak

heeheehee heeheeheehee

🎁 a homemade **cake**—with dog poop filling

🎁 a **gift certificate** for ten extra help sessions with Mrs. Crabbert

🎁 a **doll** with zits

Horses stink

🎁 a **t-shirt** that says "Horses stink"

 Cheyenne's little
sister **Chanelle**

 my little brothers
Jacob and Simon

 some of the weird **junk** Mom always
orders from those shopping channels on TV

(for example, the
egg cracker gadget

or the **oyster glove**

or the **hair removal kit** for
silky smooth skin free of
unsightly body hair)

 my **recorder** that always
makes horrible noises
when you blow into it

11

Although I think I might hang on
to my recorder.

Because **weird** things happen whenever I play it.
CREEPY things even. I kinda think my recorder
might be enchanted. Which might actually come in
handy at some point. Like Bernadette's birthday
party, for instance. ☺

At recess everyone was talking about Bernadette's party. The one talking most about Bernadette's party was Bernadette. She told us that, like, *Luigi Squeegee* or whoever would be there with his new children's collection.

We're gonna do a fashion show—Emma, Maggie, and me. Then we'll do a karaoke competition. There will be amazing prizes.

Emma

Maggie

Cheyenne's eyes lit up. Cool! she cooed. She loves that kind of thing, like clothes and stars and music and stuff.

13

But Paul, from our class,
just fidgeted with his glasses
and gave a weird look.
An unhappy look. :(

He edged over to Cheyenne and me. "Did
she say hokey-pokey competition?" he asked.
It looked like he did **not** want to come to
Bernadette's birthday.
All of a sudden, I really wanted Paul
to come, too.

I've only ever been to birthdays where we did
crafts ✂ and played games ⚅.
Or went swimming 〰 .

So it would be kind of nice to have someone
there who's as clueless as I am about karaoke
competitions and stuff like that. :D

WEDNESDAY, SEPTEMBER 7

Today I was woken by Hannibal's **squawking** yet again.

I think the squawking has gotten even *worse* the last few days.

SQUAWK!

It sounds like Hannibal is trying to mimic the *hideous* sounds my recorder makes.

I tried singing

> Well, he's as free as a bird now

so that he might start making nicer sounds.

He gave me a sweet look and even **stopped** squawking.

15

So I kept singing.
Then I gave him bird food  and
he bit my finger.
So then I squawked.

SQUAWK!

SQUAWK!

Unfortunately,
Hannibal's cage has
to stay in my room
the whole time,
because Dad gets headaches
from all the **squawking.**

That's what he says, anyway.

Eighteen days left. At least. 😐

Bernadette's
birthday party

4	5	6	7	8	9	10
11	12	13	14	15	16	17
18	19	20	21	22	23	24

Hannibal goes
home!!! Woohooo!!!!!!

I was really excited for school again. 😄
But then something **terrible** happened. ☹

Mrs. Crabbert nabbed me after health class and told me that Mr. Yang urgently needs someone who plays recorder .

This came as a
HUGE SHOCK.

Because Mr. Yang is the **conductor** of the **Wilt Whatman Middle School** orchestra.

My voice got really squeaky as I tried to tell Mrs. Crabbert that I can hardly even play recorder.

squeak

And she knows that.
Because I had to play for our class once. 🙁

muahaha

Why, you'll just
have to learn!

Mrs. Crabbert said and
gave a stupid laugh. 😶

She handed me my recorder 🎵.
Where the heck did she find that? 😖
I didn't even bring it with me to school!
Honestly, this recorder is a little **CREEPY!**

SQUAWK!

Mrs. Crabbert's bag

Then I had to go to the music
room to see Mr. Yang.

My legs began
to **TREMBLE**
on the way.

I thought maybe I should shut the
bathroom door on my finger, so I
couldn't play. But I didn't dare.

I heard all the other kids out
in the schoolyard, because it
was recess. And here I had to
go see Mr. Yang.
Talk about **UNFAIR!**

Mr. Yang was dusting a tuba or something as I came in.

Aha, my new artist.

Mr. Yang

Then he laughed with his front teeth, just like a squirrel, and his **goatee** waggled.

I told him I had unfortunately developed a | wood allergy > and could no longer play recorder.

hmmpf

But he didn't believe me and said I should play *a little something* for him.

Whatever, it's fine, I thought. There isn't a single *little something* I can even play, so he won't want me in his school orchestra.

I took a DEEP breath and blew into
my recorder. I tried to play extra bad,
and I think it worked.

In any case, Mr. Yang's hair went flying
off his head.

whoosh!
fwoop!!

And straight into the hole of the tuba.

I stopped playing at once, so that <u>nothing else</u> would fall off Mr. Yang.

Mr. Yang just reached inside the tuba  and pulled out his hair and put it back on.

sudden fever

It was a little crooked, and Mr. Yang's face was **beet red.** Like, with beads of sweat. It looked like he had suddenly *come down with something.* Maybe a fever.

So I figured I could leave and **never** play for him again. I slowly edged toward the door. Butt first.

door

22

But then Mr. Yang said he would see me at orchestra rehearsal next Monday at 2:30 on the dot.

And that I should practice properly between now and then.

 Then the bell rang. Recess was over.

But that's not all that happened today. So last week, Bernadette formed a squad. A girl squad.

Almost all of the girls in our class joined, except for Cheyenne and me. And one or two others.

At first we thought the squad was called
THE LAMB GIRLS. Ha! Ha!

That's what it sounded like, anyway. Then I
saw that Bernadette had written *THE GLAM
GIRLS* on her notebook. In silver marker.
With rhinestones.

But Cheyenne and I still call them
THE LAMB GIRLS.

And every time a **LAMB GIRL** walks by,
we baa like a **SHEEP.**

So I don't think we'll be joining *THE GLAM GIRLS* anytime soon.

But who cares. Today  Cheyenne and I started our **own** squad!
From now on, we are

And because two isn't exactly enough for a squad, we brought Paul on board.

Paul

Of course the first thing he wanted to know was what kind of squad it was.

The coolest squad ever, with, like, blood brothers and stuff. Bernadette's squad **doesn't** stand a chance against us! **We'll cream 'em!**

smack!!

Then Paul told us about his **treehouse**, where we can meet this afternoon.
⇨ To record our squad rules and stuff.

I think it was a **good idea** to include Paul in the squad!
His treehouse is awesome!

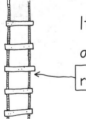

up here is the treehouse

It's way up in an oak tree and you need to climb a
[rope ladder] to get up there.

"You can pull it up when enemies are approaching," Paul said, and Cheyenne put her hands on her hips and checked it out.

Ha! Those **LAMB GIRLS** had better watch it!

Then we climbed the (ladder) and pulled it up after us.

There were a few wooden crates kicking around the treehouse and some pillows on the floor. There was even a shelf with binoculars 🔭 , some comic books 📚 , and a box with cookies 🍪 and licorice wheels. ◎ And a few bottles of apple juice. 🍶🍶

I told you it was a 😊 good idea to include Paul in the squad.

Besides, he's really smart.
You can tell by his glasses.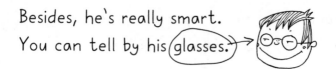

He immediately grabbed a pad of paper
and a pencil and wrote ONE FOR ALL AND
ALL FOR ONE at the top of the page.

Then we wrote down our SQUAD RULES. Paul had all the best ideas. He read everything out loud at the end.

ONE FOR ALL AND ALL FOR ONE
1. The name of the squad is THE WILD RABBITS.
2. We have no leader. ALL ARE EQUAL!
3. We have an awesome SECRET LANGUAGE and SECRET CODE!
   (We'll come up with those later.)
4. WE ALWAYS STICK TOGETHER
   (against Lamb Girls and teachers, for example!)
5. We keep each other's SECRETS!
6. We'll figure out what **THE LAMB GIRLS** are up to in their squad and SABOTAGE their activities.
7. We are NICE to old people (except Mrs. Lopez), the weak, small children and animals (unless they're squawking nymph beasts), but MERCILESS to our enemies!
8. We DON'T LAUGH AT PEOPLE just because they wear glasses, can't play recorder, or are bad at math. Unless they're NOT a member of THE WILD RABBITS.
9. Our WEAPONS are our intellect, Lotta's recorder, and whatever we can do to annoy people!

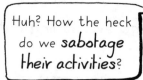

Huh? How the heck do we **sabotage their activities**?

But Paul just said he would come up with an awesome secret (secretly) language and create a WILD RABBITS binder.  And that we should start spying on **THE LAMB GIRLS** at once and record our observations.

But as Cheyenne and I were walking home, I realized how **weird** it was how much Paul had decided himself, even though we don't have a leader in THE WILD RABBITS.

Cheyenne looked as though she wanted to run back and beat Paul up.
But then she let it go.

That evening, I remembered I was supposed to practice recorder. For orchestra. I totally **freaked out** and felt **SICK** to my stomach.

I ran up to my room. On the way, I tripped over Webster, our  turtle.

Webster

(I'll write more about Webster later. I'm feeling way too **QUEASY** right now.)

When I got to my room,
Hannibal smiled at me really
nicely, with his little **red cheeks**.
He did look pretty cute, ▷
so I told him what a
beautiful bird he is.

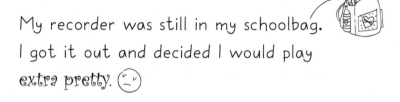

My recorder was still in my schoolbag.
I got it out and decided I would play
extra pretty. 😕

But then I thought about Mr. Yang and his
hair 🌿 again. 😊 And I laughed so hard
that my recorder just made this awful
cheeping sound.

cheep

It really hurt
my ears, but I
couldn't stop
laughing. 😄

ow!

heeheehee

cheepcheepcheep

But then Hannibal **squawked.** It sounded just as awful as my recorder. And then again. Only this time, it sounded like a sheep baa-ing.

Hannibal cocked his head to the side, like he was trying to eavesdrop. Then he baa-ed again and again. I think he liked it.

I did too, actually. I really wanted to pet him, but I was a little **scared** he'd bite me again.

So I told him what a good
little sheep he was, and
that he should feel free
to stay that way. Then
I scattered some birdfeed
for him.

But I think Hannibal thought he really had
turned into a sheep. He wouldn't eat—all
he would do was baa and baa.
Even his expression was a little
sheep-like. So. . . **blank.**

THURSDAY, SEPTEMBER 8

Cheyenne wasn't at school today. I didn't mind that much, because we had a math test.

No Cheyenne

In which case it's way better to sit next to Paul, than to Cheyenne. ☺

We stick together. ONE FOR ALL AND ALL FOR ONE. You can copy me and I can copy you.

On the double!

But then Mrs. Crabbert came to our table and told me

to go back to my seat, on the double. **OH MAN!**

In the afternoon, I wanted to go over to Cheyenne's to bring her ← homework.

But before I could, she showed up at my house, because she doesn't want her mother to find out she wasn't at school. She skipped because of math!

Omigosh!

yawn

But I need a note for school. Do you think **your** mom would write me one?

NOTE

I told her it wasn't a good idea to ask Mom. But Cheyenne pestered me for so long that I finally caved.

But Mom really said **NO** and went on a huge rant.

cranky face →

She made her **cranky** face and said that honestly, she should call Cheyenne's mother to let her know. And what was the world coming to, when you had fifth graders already playing hooky.

She was probably in such a bad mood because she had just unpacked her new **Mr. Frost** ❄ professional ice maker. And it didn't fit in the kitchen, because it was as big as a washing machine.

Then she muttered something about *"up to twenty kilos of ice cubes per day"* and stumbled over the bubble wrap  that was lying all over the kitchen.

 As if Cheyenne and I could help it, that the stuff she always buys takes up so much **space.**

Still, we made ourselves scarce and ran outside. "This is a case for **THE WILD RABBITS.**" I growled darkly, nodding, and it really did sound pretty darn important.

 I think Cheyenne was also pretty happy that we had a squad now that took care of tricky situations like this.

 Paul said, as he opened the door for us.

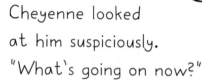

Cheyenne looked at him suspiciously. "What's going on now?"

"It's our new secret language," Paul explained. "Ourag nag-e-wag sag-e-crag-e-tag—" "Ugh, that's too hard! No one can understand you," Cheyenne interrupted, and Paul looked all offended.

Up in the treehouse, he was still looking at us all moody, with his arms all twisted up over his chest.

So, what have you found out about **THE LAMB GIRLS?** he asked, all **snotty**.

We've got a new problem on our hands! I first explained to him. Because he didn't even know that Cheyenne had played hooky and needed a note.

And this is my problem, how?

Hey! He seems to have forgotten that **we're a squad!**

ONE FOR ALL AND ALL FOR ONE!!!

So Paul had to help.

41

First we wanted to write that Cheyenne had had an orthodontist appointment, but that doesn't take all morning. Then we wanted to write that she was sick, but that usually lasts longer.

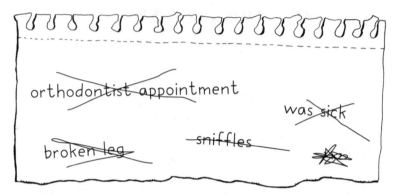

orthodontist appointment

was sick

broken leg   sniffles

Paul then went into the house to get cookies . Probably because he felt a responsibility to the squad.

Paul really comes through with the cookies.

Bring some soda, too!

Cheyenne hollered after him.

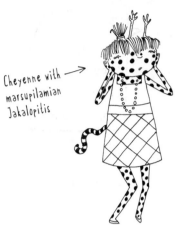
Cheyenne with marsupilamian Jakalopitis

Meanwhile, it occurred to me that what we had to do was come up with a rare disease that Mrs. Crabbert had never heard of.

Not something normal like a cold or broken leg. Something where she wouldn't know if the sickness only lasted a day.

We racked our brains, and when Paul got back, he also helped us think. He opened the cookies at the same time. But he must have forgotten the soda.

Stomachache!

he suggested, but Cheyenne didn't really like that.

43

She just rolled
her eyes.

That's
exactly the
type of boring
thing we didn't
want, dummy!

And Paul got all offended again.

But then I had **a
really good idea!**

Plague!
That's
really rare!

Paul said it was the **worst** idea
he'd ever heard, but I think he
was just jealous, because it was
my idea and not his.

In any case, he was suddenly in a **really
bad mood** and didn't want to help us
write the note anymore. He just sat
there and shoved his face with cookies.

crunch

Even though we're a squad! **Come on, Paul.**

So I just did it.

Ta-da!

Dear Mrs. Crabbert,
Cheyenne couldn't come to school yesterday,
because she came down with a little plague.
But it's better now.
Best wishes, Sandra

"How do you spell Warwick?" I asked
Cheyenne. Because that's her last name.

~~WAF~~
~~WAWRCZ~~
~~WAve~~

Cheyenne started to spell it but she wasn't
entirely sure herself because her name is so
hard. We decided to eat
a cookie for strength.

Paul just kept snorting all **stupid** the whole time and slapping himself in the forehead.

slap! slap!

But who cares. Grownups always scribble their signatures so crazy anyway that you can't even read them.

Dear Mrs. Crabbert,
Cheyenne couldn't come to school yesterday, because she came down with a little plague. But it's better now.
Best wishes, Sandra

In any case, Cheyenne was pleased with the note. Even if there were quite a lot of cookie crumbs on it.

Paul obviously still needs to learn how things work in a squad.

He got over it a little later 😊 and we
decided to ambush **THE LAMB GIRLS**.
Paul went and got his secret spy case. 🧳

There was a fingerprint dusting kit and a pipe
that you could use to look around corners, and
stuff like that. **So cool!**

Paul told us all about

sneaking up on things

and camouflage

bush

sneaky tip-toeing

and snooping 🔍 and stuff.

I think he's pretty happy to have a squad for all
his squad stuff now. 😊

Then the AMBUSH began. First we went over to Bernadette's. It was only two streets away.

Bernadette lives in a big yellow house with a huge yard. Talk about luck: Bernadette was out in the yard when we got there. Together with Emma and Maggie and Hannah, who are all **LAMB GIRLS**.

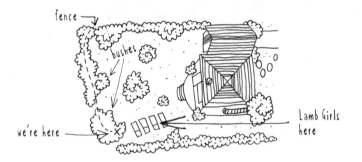

We climbed over the fence and crept through the bushes, till we were right by them.

THE LAMB GIRLS were laying on lawn chairs and looking through magazines. They would show each other the pictures of what they thought was cool and **totally crazy** and sooo cute.

Then Emma took out her lip gloss and said it tasted like cherry cola.

49

And they all tried it.

Cherry-cola-flavored Bernadette and Lamb Girls

They went back to their magazines, and Bernadette said she
wanted a pair of sunglasses
like the ones in the picture for
her birthday.

And Hannah said she wanted
the shoes  from her
magazine.

And Maggie wanted such
a t-shirt.

We crept back out through the bushes. Except Paul, I needed to nudge him a little first. He was crouched in front of me, and I think he fell asleep for a second. 😊

When we were back out on the street, we just looked at each other. Then I asked,

Why do they even have a gang, if all they do is sit around looking through magazines?

shrug

shrug

Cheyenne and Paul didn't know either. But since **THE LAMB GIRLS** were so boring, THE WILD RABBITS had the rest of the afternoon off. 😃

Right before our first class, Cheyenne handed in her note to Mrs. Crabbert.

Plague

Mrs. Crabbert read it and then gave Cheyenne a long look.

Cheyenne gave a little cough.

cough

Yeah, but I'm better now.

And then Mrs. Crabbert said she'd be calling her mother today. 😐

Cheyenne totally **freaked out!**

I almost think Paul saw this coming. That he knows you can't trick teachers, I mean. 🙂

Honestly, he could have said something.

SATURDAY, SEPTEMBER 10

Today was **BERNADETTE'S BIRTHDAY PARTY!** Mom drove Cheyenne and me and our tent and our birthday present over.

The present she got for Bernadette was a heated eyelash curler.

Shapes, separates, and defines lashes using heat

Oh man, typical Mom! What a **strange thing** to get a girl turning eleven! But absolutely <u>perfect</u> for Bernadette!!!

Although Cheyenne immediately said she wanted something like that for her birthday too.

flutter

We set up our tent in Bernadette's yard, pretty far to the side, where there were lots of bushes and a few big trees. Most of our class was already there. And everyone had really cool tents!

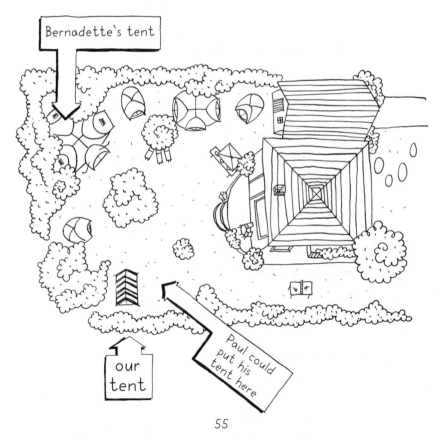

Bernadette's tent

our tent

Paul could put his tent here

Dad had given me his old tent, which he got for his birthday back when he was still a kid.

musty smell, blech!

It has orange and <u>brown stripes</u> and is made of this heavy material that smells really **musty** when you climb in.

We tossed in our things and first took a look around.

Cheyenne immediately spotted Kevin.
Kevin is Bernadette's brother and is already in ninth grade. He's the coolest boy in school. Has long hair and stuff. Lots of girls have a crush on him. Cheyenne included, naturally.

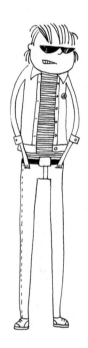

He was setting up a **massive** tent with his father. It was silver and pink and as big as an RV. It had to be where Bernadette and her *LAMB GIRLS* would be sleeping.

Bet you they even have a toilet in there. Plus a TV and a Wii.

heeheehee

Cheyenne nudged me.

The tent was set up in the far corner of the yard, not too far from ours.
A few bushes and another *LAMB GIRL* tent were all that separated us.

Then Cheyenne whispered
to me, that she wanted
to sneak up on Kevin and
yell "Boo!"

But as she was sneaking up on him, she tripped
over a tent string.

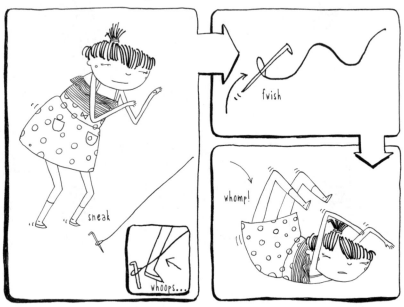

The stake was pulled out of the ground, then
she fell into the pink-and-silver tent, and the
whole thing collapsed.

Kevin looked SUPER ANNOYED, because now he and his father had to set everything back up.

woofwoofgruntwoof
woofwoofwoof
gruntwoof

Pompey and Pugsley were barking like crazy the entire time. Those are the pugs that belong to Bernadette and her family. They barked and growled at Cheyenne and looked very cute doing so.

Then Paul got there and unpacked his tent next to ours. We tried to help him pitch it, but before we knew it, all of the tent strings had formed a giant knot— and all by themselves.

Then he said he'd rather pitch his tent himself.

Paul had his own tent, because of course he needed room for all of his secret spy gear. He had brought the briefcase , along with stink bombs , a whoopee cushion (FART!), and walkie-talkies.

Cool! Paul took one walkie-talkie and Cheyenne and I took the other. In case we lost contact.

Plus we each stowed a couple of stink bombs in our pockets.

And now we must reconnoiter the premises!

wagwagwag

And that's exactly what we did.

THE WILD RABBITS

Cheyenne reconnoitered the desserts table first. And what she found was a huge pink cake with a horse on top. It was under this big angular umbrella in the shade.

ladaaa!

"Bet you it's marzipan," Cheyenne said, breaking a leg off the horse. And it was. So Cheyenne broke off another leg, because she **totally loves** marzipan. Then the horse tipped over and face-planted into the icing. So we thought we'd better scoot.

mash

plop

We finally found
Bernadette by a
staircase leading up
to the patio and her
huge yellow house.
She was playing
badminton with some
of **THE LAMB
GIRLS**. ⊖

Others were lounging
on deckchairs in the
yard.

Most of the boys were
roughhousing around a
big ping-pong table and
fighting over who got
to play. Only no one
was actually playing,
because everyone
was fighting.

biff!

thump!

Then there was cake 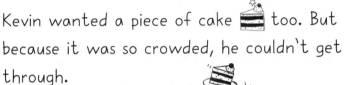 and more cake and cookies. The whole class swarmed the desserts table and loaded up their plates.

Cheyenne took mostly chocolate-covered marshmallows, 'cause those are her favorite.

Kevin wanted a piece of cake too. But because it was so crowded, he couldn't get through.

The desserts are behind the crowd!

Kevin

So Cheyenne helped him. Or at least, she tried.

Unfortunately, she bumped into the table and one of the stink bombs in her skirt pocket broke.

She smelled so bad afterward, that no one came near us.
Or the desserts.

Kevin wasn't in the mood for cake now, either.

Then the *fashion show* kicked off. It was so **borinG,** because it was just Bernadette, Emma, and Maggie walking across the yard on this long carpet. With different clothes on each time.

Luigi Squeegee or what-ever his name is, was talking into the mic, describing the clothes, and then he'd turn up the music **really louD.**

With all that racket, we couldn't hear the beeping and crackling of our walkie-talkies.

cracklecrackbeeeeep

stink eye

So we had to **SCREAM** into them, to drown out the other noise. Bernadette really gave us the stink eye for that.

But then things got a bit more interesting, because now it was time for the karaoke competition. Bernadette stood at the top of the patio stairs and held up something small and green.

???

!!!

A **mini MP3 player!** Two gigabytes of storage. Can be clipped to a backpack or clothing! This is the grand prize for our karaoke competition!

AHHH!

Everyone started screaming, myself included, because I definitely wanted to win that!

There's no way I'll ever get an MP3 player from my parents, because Dad's unfortunately stuck in the Stone Age. He still thinks a telephone has to have a cord.

"We'll sing something together," Cheyenne said instantly, which I didn't really like at first.

Because then there'd be two of us, and there's only <u>one</u> MP3 player. ☹

But then I said yes, because Cheyenne has a nice voice. ☺

My grandma once told me I sound like **a duck with the hiccups** when I sing.

We wanted to check out the songbook, but a clucking clutch of **LAMB GIRLS** was already there.

Of course Bernadette went first. She stood at the top of the stairs and danced and tossed her hair and sang something in French.

singing in French

tossing

dancing

She was totally showing off which made me even crankier. Because she probably wanted to win the MP3 player herself, which was not very host-like of her.

Cheyenne was **mad** too. She yanked the songbook away from  Hannah and we sat down behind a bush.

yank!!

grrrrr

Cheyenne looked for something for us to sing.

Calling Paul, over!

Meanwhile, I spoke into the walkie-talkie, because Paul had vanished. And I wanted to know where he was.

But he had locked himself in the bathroom and said he wasn't coming out till the competition was over. And that we should go ahead and sing without him.

RESTROOM

Paul here, over!

Cheyenne liked a lot of the songs. But they had names like **Pigs Don't Fly** or **Viva la Frida,** and I didn't know any of them.

Then we finally found one I knew, but only because I had it on cassette tape from when I was a baby.

We practiced behind the bush, and changed up the lyrics a bit.

That is, until Cheyenne said it might be best if I just moved my lips → during our turn, or clapped my hands and let her do the singing.

ARRRGH!

That made me **really maD!** I jumped up and ran to our tent. But Cheyenne followed me.

Hey man, all I wanted to do was help!

she said and crouched next to me on my sleeping bag.

71

And then she promised I would get the MP3 player, if we won, because she already has one.

It was **so nice** of her and made me really happy! Cheyenne is **my best friend**, pure and simple! :)

But I brought my recorder along, just to be safe. After all, an MP3 player is on the line.

Emma and Maggie were currently up. It might've been best if Maggie had just moved her lips too.

Cheyenne shouted **BOOO!** really **loud.** I didn't think that was too smart, though, because we were next.

In any case, as we stood at the top of the stairs, **THE LAMB GIRLS** were giving us this weird look. Like **aGGressive,** somehow.

lame (or lamb!) look

Then the music started and we had to sing.

CLAP!
CLAP!

I felt so **QUEASY,** that I couldn't do more than move my lips, after all. But Cheyenne sang really well and even danced along.

But **THE LAMB GIRLS** still yelled **BOOO!** and laughed out lamb.

Then Pompey and Pugsley climbed the stairs and barked at us.

They just stood there the whole time and **growled** and **howled** and **scowled**
and Bernadette
and **THE LAMB GIRLS**
and the boys almost died laughing.

That made me so **mad!!!** I whipped out my
recorder and blew into
it! The sounds that came
out were not
suitable for dogs'
ears.  ᶜʳʳʳʳ

In any case, Pompey
and Pugsley dashed off,
whimpering.

squeesqueee →

Cheyenne kept singing and dancing the whole
time, even though it had also started to rain.

Bernie had some little lambs,
little lambs, little lambs,
Bernie had some little lambs . . .

Everywhere that **BERNIE** went
the lambs were
sure to go

patter

What's weird is that it was only raining 🌧 on us, up on the stairs. Our whole class was dry, ☀ standing in the yard and gawking at the way Cheyenne kept singing and dancing, as we kept getting **WETTER**.

Even Kevin was there, gawking. That made Cheyenne sing and dance and twirl around even better.

clapsplash

I was clapping, which sent raindrops flying through the air.

76

I couldn't help but think that it's high time I figured out what the deal is with my recorder.

Maybe I'll go ask at the specialty shop where Mom bought it. It's just not normal that every time I blow into it, something **strange** happens! It's almost like magic.

When we came down the patio stairs after finishing, Paul was back.

Now it's your turn Cheyenne said, wringing out her hair. "Even though that MP3 player is as good as ours."

Paul just shook his head. "No way," he said, shaking his head like his life depended on it. "I'd rather spend the rest of the day locked in the bathroom."

Almost none of the other boys sang, either, so the competition was over pretty fast. I was so excited for the prize-giving, but sadly, Hannah won the MP3 player. **Pretty obvious, right?** A **LAMB GIRL,** who else would it be?!

Cheyenne, Paul, and I just did WILD RABBIT stuff after that. We spied on **THE LAMB GIRLS** and used our walkie-talkies.

Paul stood behind an oak tree and Cheyenne and I hid in a bush.

They're sitting together on the stairs. Now they're looking suspiciously toward your bush and giggling like idiots. I bet they're planning something **secret!**

Paul

Cheyenne and I are in here

We need to sneak up on them.

And that's what we did. Also,

1. we **CAMOUFLAGED** ourselves. For that, we needed to snap a few branches off the bush, but Bernadette's mother still spotted us and got mad.

2. Cheyenne put the **WHOOPEE CUSHION** on Bernadette's mother's chair. Man, was that a fart!

FART!

3. Paul eavesdropped on ***THE LAMB GIRLS*** with a **BUGGING DEVICE.**

4. The Lamb Girls **DISCOVERED** the bug and **squawked** into it. Paul was deaf for half an hour after that. 😐

huh?

5. The **Rockers** **STOLE** our spy case. 🙁

80

The Rockers are another squad. It's Matthew, Finn, Tim, and Benny, the strongest boys in our class.

They found our squad rules in the briefcase, and Tim read them out loud. **"The WilD Rabbits, haha!"** the others roared.

This is a case for... **us!**

Revenge!

shaking her fist

huh?

"Huh?" Paul asked, because he was still a little deaf.

But revenge had to wait, because
first came dinner.

A catering service arrived in two
cars, and they set up tons of
food on a long table.

Cheyenne's eyes  lit up, but
once we took a closer look,
she got really quiet.

Hey, where's
the ketchup?

There were all these **WEIRD**
things on the table. You
couldn't really tell if it was
WORMS or **SNAILS**
or **FRIED DOG POOP** *eeeewww!*
—or something you could
actually eat.

???
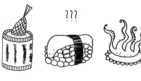

Oh man. I don't think they like us here. They're
trying to poison us.

Luckily, Bernadette has a cat. One of those
FLOOFY LONG-HAIRED ones.

 Her name is **Poppy,** and she's very
trusting. And pretty hungry too.

Only Cheyenne couldn't remember
her name and kept calling her **Potty.**
But I think she kind of did it on purpose.

Cheyenne and Paul and I
each got a plate of food
and went with Poppy
to our tent.

And whatever tasted **WEIRD** went to Poppy.

snail?
weird
worms?
rabbit poop
weird

Poppy ran off at some point, but by then we'd
eaten almost everything up.

There were just a few small
rolls left on Cheyenne's plate.
She didn't like them , because they were
filled with little bits of brown stuff. She had
to go look for a **trashcan,** since Poppy was gone.

Mrs. Besler's fancy handbag

Luigi Squeegee

Bernadette's riding helmet

Lamb Girl tent

Later on, Bernadette started yelling about who
had dumped all the pierogis into
the bidet in the bathroom.

Cheyenne was scared to go to the bathroom
after that, because she didn't know what a
bidet was. (Neither did Paul or I, actually.)
Besides, she'd always thought that **pierogis**
were, like, little animals that bite.

Even though Paul thought they were probably
one of the **weird** dishes served.

Then Bernadette started yelling
some more, because Poppy had
puked in her sleeping bag.
Man, what **yelling!**

There was a **DANCE**
after dinner, but
Cheyenne, Paul, and I
didn't have time for that.

We sat outside our tent and crafted plans for
the **NIGHT OF** THE WILD RABBITS. We had a lot
ahead of us.

waaaaaaaaah

Paul wrote everything down:

1. We'll sneak to the **Rockers'** tent and **STEAL BACK THE BRIEFCASE.**

2. We'll plant a **STINK BOMB** while we're there.

3. Then we'll sneak to **THE LAMB GIRLS'** tent and make **CREEPY SOUNDS.**

    booohoo hiss

4. Once everyone's up and scared, Lotta will blow <u>as hard as</u> she can into her **RECORDER.**

5. And then something really **CREEPY** will happen!!!

    creepy sheepy

Eventually, Bernadette's mother told us to get in our tents.
Paul crawled into his.

Cheyenne and I stayed up
for a long time, because we
had to wait till everyone
fell asleep.

Unfortunately, everyone else was up for a long
time too. We ended up dozing off at some
point. 😴 😴

Then suddenly, something was
scratching 👁 👁 at our
tent. It was pitch dark ▪️
and we heard some night
birds who-who-ing.

scritchscratch

WHO!
WHO!

Wtto
Wtto

scritchscratch

I was nearly scared to **death.**

Till Paul said it was just him.

Cheyenne would have liked to wallop him, but then Paul quickly said that

THE WILD RABBITS had to stick together, and ⟶ ONE FOR ALL AND ALL FOR ONE.

So of course Cheyenne couldn't hit him.

I would have preferred to stay in my sleeping bag, which was really cozy.
But we had to exact revenge.
For karaoke 🏓 and pierogis 🐤 and stealing our briefcase. 💼

We could not let Bernadette get away with that! Much less the **Rockers!!!**

So we snuck up to the **Rockers'** tent. Or at least, we tried to. But it was so dark ▮ that we could barely see.

I tripped over a tent string 🪝 and Cheyenne crashed straight into a tree.

We completely lost our way and **couldn't** find the tent. 😑

So we decided to look for Bernadette, Emma, and Maggie's tent, to scare them. Theirs was so **big,** it had to be easier to find.

But I was really **scared,** because it was **pitch dark** and the night birds were making such **creepy** sounds!

"Here it is," Paul whispered at some point.

We stopped in our tracks, and I took a deep breath. Then I blew into the recorder.

It sounded worse than all the night birds put together!

We turned and tried to run, but there were all these thorny bushes standing in our way and we got caught.

Everyone in the tent started **yellinG** and **cursinG,** then the zipper opened and Matthew Finn Tim and Benny jumped out.

GGGRRRRRR!!

OH NOOO! We finally found the **Rockers'** tent!!! Only now theirs was the wrong one! The boys **swore** 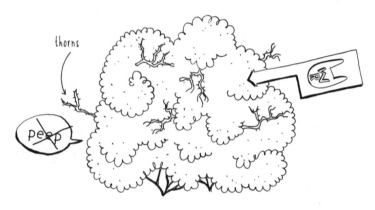 and **shook** their fists "☞" "☞" and **ran** back and forth and **hollered** about what they'd do when they caught **the** culprit.

thorns

We were lucky it was so dark. Cheyenne, Paul, and I were caught in the bushes and didn't make a peep.

Wanna bet it was Lotta with her recorder?

Then they all shouted stuff about LOTTA and THE WILD RABBITS and **REVENGE.**

The **Rockers** took off into the darkness, heading in the general direction of our tent. One would occasionally bellow "**OW!**" because they had forgotten a flashlight.

We stayed in the bushes till the "**OW**"s grew quieter. It took a really long time to get out, and I lost about half of my **PJs** →
to the thorns.

Then we crept into the **Rockers'** tent and got the spy case. Luckily we found the flashlight right off, otherwise we might have taken Tim's CD player by accident.

Later, when the **Rockers** were back in their
tent, we slinked back to our tents too.
Only there were no longer any tents
to speak of, just piles of fabric.

The stakes had also vanished.
Paul looked around with the
flashlight ◌▭, and that's when I noticed he
<u>wasn't</u> wearing his glasses ⊘⊗. Well, now
we knew why he took us to the <u>wrong</u> tent!

AW man, Paul! He's
got **a lot** to learn,
if he wants to be
a **real member**
of our squad!

We dug out our sleeping bags and Paul's glasses
from the tent piles and
slept under a bush.

It was actually really nice. And not even that cold. Then Paul pointed out different constellations, and I got really sleepy 😴 😴 . I think it was around **Cassiopeia** that my eyes closed. 😴 😴

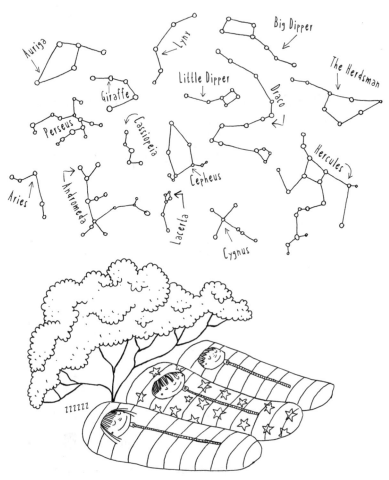

I didn't wake up 😴 😴 again till it started to rain. 🌧️

SUNDAY, SEPTEMBER 11

When I snuck into the house this
morning, I was **FREEZING** cold and
my throat was on fire.

What burned me even more was to discover that
THE LAMB GIRLS had all snuggled up and
slept on mattresses in the living room. They
actually went inside, those Wimps!

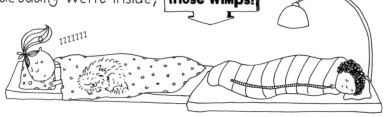

Mom **finally** came to pick me up later.
All I wanted was to go home, get
in bed, and sleep for hours.

KABOOM

Sadly, it was still raining and
my brothers were playing **moon
feud** or something
in their room. 😑
And their room is right next to mine. 😲

Or maybe they were playing **Airplane Crash** or the **Sinking of the Titanic**. Whatever it was, the game called for them to jump from their dresser to the floor and pound on pots and pans with soup ladles.

AaaarrGh! EiGht-year-olD brothers shoulD be outlaweD!!! 💀

Mom kicked them out at some point and I finally fell asleep ☻ ☻. In almost no time, I was up again ☻ ☻ because Hannibal was **SQUAWKiNG!** I quickly gave him some birdfeed, so he'd zip it. I think he forgot he's actually a sheep now.

birdie nom nom

SQUAWK! =

Cheyenne came over that afternoon, and we tried to think of something fun to do, because it was still raining.

Then Cheyenne came up with the **idea** of teaching Hannibal how to speak.

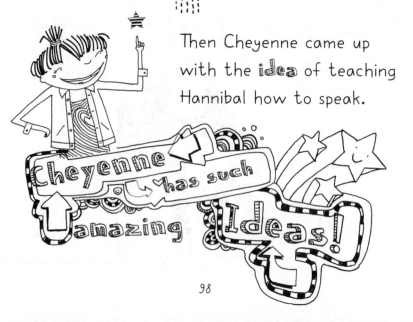

Cheyenne has such amazing Ideas!

Funny, that I hadn't thought of that yet!

I started things off, saying

to Hannibal.

Hannibal cocked his head and gave me a cute look. Almost as if he were consider-ing baa-ing a bit again.

Cheyenne is cool!

Which made Hannibal squawk so bad, the window panes in my room began to rattle.

He must not have thought Cheyenne was that cool.

I plugged my ears and screamed

LOTTA iS COOOOOOOL!

And then Dad came upstairs and kicked us out, even though it was still raining. He **ranted** on about how, even on a Sunday, he can't get away from **noisy** brats. Dad's a teacher, after all.

Out!

Talk about **Unfair!** We get kicked out, while Hannibal gets to stay inside. He's the noisiest brat of all!

After grumbling a bit, we went over to Paul's. Because hanging out in Paul's treehouse in the rain had to beat standing around outside our house.

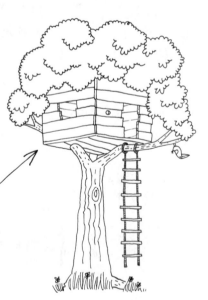

Paul was home, and his mother even gave us cookies  before we climbed into the treehouse.

Paul is a a **really valuable member** for a squad like ours, even if he could stand to learn a few things.

I had brought my recorder and we decided I should practice a little. To make the recorder do things to annoy **THE LAMB GIRLS**. Like making their pen leak during a dictation or something.

I started practicing, and Cheyenne immediately dropped the bowl of cookies.

The cookies were round,
the kind with jam
in the middle that I
don't actually like that much.

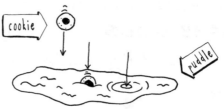

They rolled to the door and fell out. Sadly,
there wasn't any grass right underneath the
treehouse, just a kind of crater with a big
puddle. And that's exactly where the cookies
landed.

[cookie]

[puddle]

Paul got all **grumpy** and said I
should test my recorder on **THE
LAMB GIRLS** directly—and
not on his favorite cookies.

Cheyenne agreed.

So we climbed down and went over to Bernadette's. But of course no one was outside, because it was still raining. The yard was **completely back to normal,** as if a birthday party had never taken place here yesterday.

That's why we decided to go back to the treehouse. ⬅️➡️

Along the way, we spotted a group of boys headed toward us. It was the **Rockers.**

Paul got a little **NERVOUS**, but Cheyenne said I could practice just as well on them.

We quickly hid **behind** a nearby bus stop shelter.

Then, as the **Rockers** passed, I blew into my recorder. It **squeaked** pretty bad.

At that very moment, the rain gutter on the shelter kinked, and all of the water came splashing down on the **Rockers.** They **hollered** and **screamed** like crazy.

Lucky that we were hidden behind the shelter!

But then Cheyenne
started giggling so loud,
that the **Rockers** heard her.

HEEHEEHEE!

WE HAD TO BOOK IT OUT OF THERE.

We ran as fast as we could.

But the **Rockers**
were faster.

Riiiiiiiiiiiiiiiiiiiiiiiinnngg!

phew!

Luckily, Paul's house was
nearby, and we rang the
doorbell like crazy, so the
Rockers stopped chasing us.

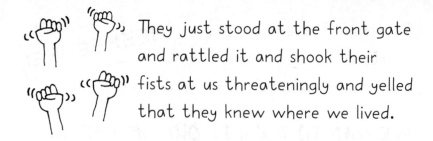 They just stood at the front gate and rattled it and shook their fists at us threateningly and yelled that they knew where we lived.

I hope they don't know where **I** live, I thought, but I kept it to myself.

Nitwit!

Paul was in a **terrible mood** again. He didn't even want to let Cheyenne into the house, and said she was the biggest **nitwit** of all time and should just go home.

ONE FOR ALL AND ALL FOR ONE!

But Paul still wanted her to leave. I went with her, although we did wait till all of the **Rockers** were out of sight.

But Paul really Does have a few thinGs to learn, if he Wants to stay in the squaD!!!

MONDAY, SEPTEMBER 12

Hannibal's **squawking** woke me up again. But that's nothing new at this point.

SQUAWK!

Lotta is cool! I said to him, and he **squawked** back. But maybe he was just trying to repeat after me.

SQUAWK!

So I tried it again, saying "Lottttttaaaaaa isssss cooool!" really slow.

Huh?

slap!

But then I completely **FREAKED OUT.**

Because I suddenly remembered that I had **ORCHESTRA REHEARSAL** this afternoon!

And I <u>haven't</u> practiced recorder at all in the past few days! Other than at the karaoke competition 🏸 and the thing with the cookies ⬤ and with the **Rockers** "✊", that is. But I don't think that counts for Mr. Yang. ☹

I couldn't really concentrate at school, because I was thinking of ORCHESTRA REHEARSAL the whole time.

And now, Lotta will perform everything she practiced. Hehehehehe!

And it didn't help when Mrs. Crabbert told the whole class during math, that two students from 5b were now in orchestra.

That would be Bernadette and me.

On the contrary: I felt **SICK** to my stomach! I had forgotten that Bernadette plays in the school orchestra too.

She turned around and gave me this look. All stuck-up. And she gave me a **nasty** smile. And whispered something to Emma. Because she knows full well that I can't even play recorder. 😑

psspsspss

I thought about getting sick. I had a **STOMACHACHE,** after all.

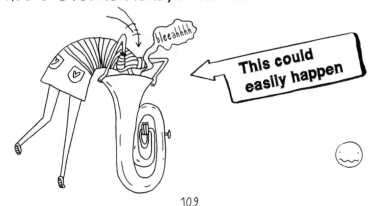

bleeahhhh

This could easily happen

But then Bernadette
would probably tell
everyone I was afraid.

So I had to go.

Maybe I could do the same thing
as in the karaoke competition.
Just move my fingers and
pretend to play.

If only Cheyenne were there! But she doesn't
need to learn an instrument. She gets to play
video games ⌐═╛ while I'm at rehearsal.
So unfair!

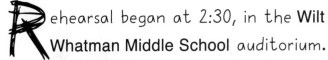

Rehearsal began at 2:30, in the **Wilt Whatman Middle School** auditorium. Besides me, there were only two girls who played flute  and we had to practice together.

One of them was named Fiona and she was already in ninth grade. She had glasses and braces. And she was really bossy.

Fiona

glasses

braces

flute

ninth

paper

She gave me this piece of paper with musical notes ♫ ♩ ♩ on it and told me to play.

Honestly, to me, sheet music looks like a fly **pooped** on a piece of paper. I never know what the notes are supposed to be.

If it said Jingle Bells or something at the top of the page, I'd at least know what song I had to play.
But instead it said *Concertino in C Major.*

What the heck is that?

So I just blew into the recorder and moved my fingers around a little. It didn't sound all that bad. It was kinda like Dad's computer, which beeps when you turn it on.

But Fiona still plugged her ears and glared at me. I think she wanted to complain too, but her braces had gotten caught somehow and she couldn't open her mouth.

All she could manage was "ng, ng, ng."

So Mr. Yang sent her home and said her mother should take her to the orthodontist.

And then Mr. Yang said he actually
just wanted to practice with Bernadette,
because she's playing the violin solo.

But since Fiona was gone, now he wanted me
to play something too. ⊖
The beginning of the *Concertino in C Major*, no less.

I was even more NERVOUS than before,
mainly because Bernadette gave me
this strange smile. And Mr. Yang
grabbed onto his hair.

← strange smile

I concentrated on the sheet music as hard
as I could. Then I started to play—only I didn't
get far. ♩♪♩

No, no, no!

Mr. Yang bellowed,
pulling on his hair. His
goatee waggled too.

All because I goofed a little.
It can happen.

Then he asked me what the heck I thought
I was playing.

I looked at the
piece of paper
covered in notes
and said:

Concertino in
C Major?

Bernadette **totally laughed** her head off and Mr. Yang took away my recorder and said Bernadette would now show me what the *Concertino in C Major* sounds like.

ababa babaaa

I thought it was **really uncool** that Bernadette got to play my recorder, but on the other hand, she was in for the shock of her life. **Ha!**
I moved back a few steps to take cover, just in case.

Then Bernadette started to play and I thought she must have secretly grabbed a different instrument. It didn't sound anything like my recorder. It was more like when a bird sings. When it **trillerts,** or whatever the word is.

$\mathcal{A}$nd then something else happened. So, the windows in the auditorium were open, and all of a sudden, a few birds flew in  and landed on the music stand. And then a couple more. There were at least fifteen or twenty. And they all began to sing. It sounded really *beautiful* together with the recorder.

But then Bernadette stopped playing, because she was so amazed. The birds ~~trillerted~~ trilled a bit more, then flew back out. One after the other.

Bernadette looked at the recorder first, then at me. As if she felt sorry for the recorder. ⊖

Mr. Yang brushed a tear from his eye, and his goatee waggled. "THAT," he proclaimed, "is music! That is the *Concertino in C Major!*"

Then he sent me home with my recorder and the sheet music and said I had to practice really hard between now and next week. ⊖

On the way home, I stopped
by Cheyenne's, because this
was clearly A CASE FOR THE
WILD RABBITS!

We show our enemies no mercy!

WE MUST PUT AN END TO EVIL!!

AN END TO ORCHESTRA REHEARSALS!!!

grrrrrr!

SuperRabbit →

Cheyenne had already finished her
homework and joined me.

We were headed
for Paul's treehouse.

← pirate rabbit

You want wild — I'll show you wild!!!!

On the way there, we spotted the **Rockers.** They were hanging around Paul's house, looking suspicious.

They're getting on my nerves.

Were they following us? Either way, we decided to approach through the backyard.

We cautiously rang the doorbell at Paul's. The wall next to the front door was covered in splotches of color. As if a box of paints had exploded or something.

Weird, they weren't there before.

Paul was still **super angry** and said we should scram and never come back.

The **WILD RABBITS** are total poop! And you two are as lame as your idiotic ideas.

Then he slammed the door shut. **WHAM!**

Can we still go up in your treehouse? Cheyenne called after him, but Paul did not respond.

Now that was really too bad. **THE WILD RABBITS** aren't half as much fun without the treehouse.

Or without Paul.

As we walked back, we decided that it might not be all that bad to just sit around as a squad and try out cherry-cola lip gloss. And look through magazines.

I found one of Mom's magazines. It's called *TRASH*. It has all these crazy stories and pictures.

About people who were abducted by **ALIENS** and stuff like that.

← UFO

I liked that idea.

And then I went home.

On the way to my room, I tripped over Webster, our turtle. (I'll write more about Webster later. I have to go practice recorder.)

TUESDAY, SEPTEMBER 13

I was really looking forward to school today, because we didn't have school. It was the SCHOOL OLYMPICS! 😄

Cheyenne was excited too, even though she's not that good at sports. Only she's worse at school.

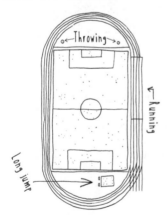

When we reached the athletics field, all of the girls in our class were standing around Bernadette, cooing and clucking.

They always do that, but today they were being extra annoying standing around and extra loud clucking . Cheyenne and I went over to take a look.

bockbock!

cackle

Bernadette was wearing new sports gear. Luigi Squeegee gear, of course. That dude from her birthday party.

Her top was the same color as my toothpaste at home, only covered in glittery stars. It was **too much.**

bling bling

"That looks **so funny**," Cheyenne whispered to me. "Bling bling. Like a Christmas tree."

♫ O Christmas tree, ♪
O Christmas tree,
How blingy are
thy branches... ♫
♩ ♩

We both started laughing. We hopped away, singing *"O Christmas Tree."* 😊

hop

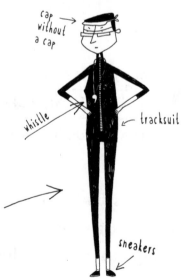

cap without a cap

whistle

tracksuit

We laughed even more when we saw Mrs. Crabbert. She had dressed up like a **real athlete,** complete with a tracksuit. 😄

sneakers

= whistle!

What's more, she was wearing one of those visor caps **without** a cap, where your hair pokes out on top. And a whistle around her neck. She blew into it and our class had to line up.

She had a schedule ⟶ of when it was our class's turn for running, long jump, and throwing. Bernadette was put in charge of the sheet, obviously.

Then she went over to the landing pit, because she had to measure the distances.

Mrs. Crabbert's measuring tape for long jump

Haha!
2 ft.

Excuse me?
2.5 ft

Forget it!
3 ft

Whoa
3.5 ft

Almost...
4 ft

Keep Practicing!
4.5 ft

Something happen?
5 ft

Well...
5.5 ft

Speechless
6 ft

Bernadette acted all important and called out:

First up is long throw! Everyone line up in pairs!

But **THE LAMB GIRLS** were the only ones who lined up in pairs.

WÖÖÖöööÖö!!!!!

Everyone else took off screaming. Cheyenne and myself included.

At the throwing area, we had to line up alphabetically. Bernadette was near the very front, of course, because her last name starts with **"B."** I was pretty far back, but Cheyenne was almost at the end of the line.

A B C D E ... N O P ... U V W ... Z

Bernadette   Lamb Girls   me   Maggie

Bernadette turned around
and gave us a stuck-up look.

> Well, I can see
> we're already
> lined up perfectly
> for the awards.

bockbocckbockbockbock

And those annoying
LAMB GIRLS started
cackling again.

All except Maggie hmpf because her last name
is Vargas, so she was right in front of Cheyenne
in line. Ha! Ha!

That made me really
mad, and I snuck back
to Cheyenne. "Obvious
case for THE WILD RABBITS."
I whispered to her.

> We have to make sure
> Bernadette doesn't win
> any awards.

Cheyenne shook her fists and growled like a tiger.

hiss!

grrrrrrr rooaaaarrrrr

 ONE FOR ALL AND ALL FOR ONE!

Even though there were only **two** of us left in the squad.

Then Mrs. Fisher, our English teacher, turned up and strongly suggested I find my way back to my spot. Then long throw got started. Everyone had three tries.

Unfortunately, Bernadette could throw pretty far. Almost 100 feet!

And there I stood in my spot in line and couldn't do a darn thing! I didn't even have my recorder along.

Paaaauuu!

When Paul's turn came, we **CHEERED LOUDLY** for him. Because maybe then he'd let us back up in the treehouse.

But Paul just turned around and hissed at us to shut our traps. Then he barely managed to throw 40 feet. **serves him riGht!**

hehehe

Benny and Matthew from the **Rockers** laughed, then both threw really far. Which made me feel bad for Paul again.

But first I had myself to worry about, because now it was my turn to throw.

THE LAMB GIRLS were all whispering to each other.

LAMB whispering

Then Cheyenne yelled out Baa! Baa! and I <u>couldn't</u> concentrate at <u>all.</u>

FIRST TRY

a bit off...

As a result, the first ball I threw hit Mr. Yang in the head. He was watching the long throw area next to us, where 7a was up.

His hair went all crooked again, and he started yelling really loud , his goatee waggling.

But it wasn't on purpose, honest! 🙁

Our whole class laughed, and I felt even more **nervous** than before.

Because of that, I only managed about 35 feet on my **SECOND TRY,** even less than Paul.

But by my **THIRD TRY,** I made it almost 50 feet.

Let's hope you can run

Bernadette said as I walked past her.

bling bling

The glittery stars ☆ on her *Luigi-Squeegee-* toothpaste-shirt glittered and **THE LAMB GIRLS** tittered.

bahahahahaaa

That made me so **MAD!**

Let's hope you didn't buy glittery pajamas too, or you'd look as stupid at night as you do during the day!

bling bling

No.1

One thing was certain:

Bernadette had to be stopped!

But first it was Cheyenne's turn to throw. She's actually pretty good at throwing. I saw it myself, the time she **broke** that window with a sour apple. Accidentally, of course.

But she must have been a bit **nervous** today.

She took a big running start and wound up the throw as she went. She probably could have thrown it really f a r.

Only Mr. Yang's head got in the way again.

trajectory
of ball

hits Mr. Yang

All because Cheyenne threw it a little *crooked*.

This time, Mr. Yang's hair fluttered down to the ground. That's because Cheyenne is stronger than me.

trajectory of hair

I think that Cheyenne wanted to apologize to Mr. Yang. But she couldn't, because she was laughing so hard. And then she was **DISQUALIFIED** and wasn't allowed to throw anymore. So **unfair!**

After that we went over to the landing pit, because **long jump** was next.

On the way, we worked out a plan for how to mess up Bernadette's jump. Cheyenne came up with **a really great idea.**

She had brought a peanut butter sandwich for snack time. She gave it to me to stick under Bernadette's sneakers.

Half the sandwich under each shoe.

Bernadette's sneakers from below with peanut butter sandwich

So I had to sneak all the way up to "**B.**" When I got there, I kneeled down and pretended to tie my shoelace. Even though my shoes are Velcro.

Velcro

Bernadette didn't see me. But then she took a step back, right onto my hand. I screamed and dropped the peanut butter sandwich.

SQUAWK!

"What are yooou doing all the way up here?"
Bernadette asked all snooty, and Finn from the
Rockers yelled out "Stupid Rabbits!"

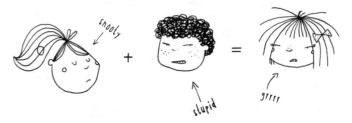

I jumped up and accidentally stepped on the
sandwich

Lotta Petermann,
back to your
spot, on the
double!

ugh

ugh

ugh

Mrs. Crabbert yelled
from the landing pit.

And everyone stared at
me, even though she
looked way sillier with
her tracksuit and the
visor cap without a cap
and her hair sticking
out on top.

I went back and the peanut butter squished under my feet with each step.

I left a trail of brown marks behind me on the track. It looked like I had stepped into a huge pile of dog poop.

When it was Bernadette's turn, Cheyenne and I yelled out [Baa! Baa!] but she still jumped twelve feet, one inch.

Whoa, so far!

And then Mrs. Crabbert
stomped over and yelled
at Cheyenne and me,
calling us unfair!

That's not true, because Bernadette
can throw and jump really far.
Plus she
plays violin **and**
recorder really well.
THAT's what's
Unfair!!!

Un fair!!!

But it was better not to say anything,
so I wouldn't be disqualified too. Then Mrs.
Crabbert went back to the landing pit. On
the way she stepped in the peanut butter
sandwich, which was in tatters by now,
leaving a trail of dog-poop-footprints on the
track too.

I jumped as far as I could, but only made it
eight feet, six inches. ☺
But that was because it was still a little
SLICK under my shoes.

Why?	Gym-bag-forgetter	Beginner
7 ft	7.5 ft	8 ft

Try it backwards...	Go home	Nope. Just nope.
8.5 ft	9 ft	9.5 ft

Cheyenne didn't even reach
the landing pit. That's
because she jumped too early.

Mrs. Crabbert told her to go to the back of
the line and try again, but Cheyenne grabbed
her foot and said she couldn't, because she had
broken her leG.

So Mrs. Crabbert simply drew a line next to Cheyenne's name on the list.

Cheyenne may have been hoping Kevin would help her up. He had been watching the landing pit too. But Kevin acted as though he had something to add to a list, and looked in the **other** direction.

START — 50 yard dash → FINISH

Certificate of Excellence

for

Bernadette Bester

awarded for exceptional performance in the Wilt Whatman Middle School Olympics

When it was our turn to run, Cheyenne's foot was doing better. That was important too, because we had to do something to **prevent** Bernadette from earning an award.

We decided to
tie her **shoelaces**
together before
the race began.

It wasn't exactly easy, though, because people
tend to notice things like that.

So Cheyenne had to distract her.
I quickly knelt down behind Bernadette
and slowly pulled on her shoelaces.

And Cheyenne bounced up and down in front of her like a bouncy ball.

Bernadette gave her this really **evil** smile.

All **THE LAMB GIRLS** started clucking and cawing.

Hehehehehehehehhehehheeheehehehehehehheeheehehehehehhehehehe

↳ Bockbockb-cawbockbockbockbockbockbockb-cawbockbockbockbock

But then Emma said:

Hey, what are you doing?

And she yanked me back by my shoulders, knocking me over, right onto a water bottle that was standing behind me on the ground. So then my **butt really hurt.**

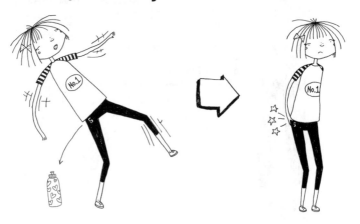

 And next it was Bernadette's turn to run. And she was *really fast*— **under eight seconds!**

I had to run at the same time as Emma and Hannah. At the starting line, both of them stomped on my heels.

Emma on my left and Hannah on my right.

That made my shoes really loose, and I couldn't fix them in time. So about ten yards into the race, I lost one of them.

But because I was *faster* than Emma and Hannah, I kept running.

fwoop!

After another ten yards or so, I lost the
other shoe too.

But I still came in

First at the finish
line.

I'm actually a pretty
fast runner! Most
importantly, *much
faster* than Hannah
and Emma.

Everyone still laughed at me, though.
HAHA!
Just because my shoes were still lying on
the track.

F I N I S H

Sadly, Cheyenne totally wiped out and didn't even make it past the starting line. 😔

whomp!

Turns out someone had tied her shoelaces together.

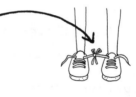

Bernadette tallied up her points and told us she was guaranteed an **award.** With a real **signature from the mayor.** She said she probably did **the best out of all the girls in our grade.** 🙁

Cheyenne growled, limping, because she had busted up her **knee.**

And she said she was gonna go eat her peanut butter sandwich .

But then she got even **madder,** because she remembered that her peanut butter sandwich was stuck to the bottom of Mrs. Crabbert's shoe. ───>

And just as she was taking it out on a fence post that got in her way on the edge of the athletic field, ────────>

we happened to discover that the **Rockers**
had buried Paul in the landing pit. Paul was
fighting back, but there wasn't much he could
do, because his head was all that poked out.
And whenever he tried to yell, they poured
sand ⋯⋯ in his mouth. Which made him **spit**
and **cough** and he **could not yell.**

Cheyenne and I looked at each other, and it was obvious what we had to do. We hissed:

ONE FOR ALL AND ALL FOR ONE!

Right at the very same time.

Then we grabbed a net that was hanging over the fence.

We took off, one on the right and one on the left. The **Rockers** didn't see us, because we were coming from behind.

REVENGE for THE RABBITS!

Cheyenne bellowed, and then we wrapped up the **Rockers** and pushed them over.

No idea where all those knots in the net came from. Anyway, the boys were **completely** trapped. 😉

They said quite a lot of **unfriendly** things to us—all except for Finn. He wasn't able to, because his face was squished somewhere between Benny's belly and Tim's butt.

Cheyenne and I dug Paul out of the pit. We wanted to brush the sand off of him, but he didn't want that.

Thanks he murmured, his face all red and his glasses *crooked* and stuff.

At that, Paul smiled
a little and nodded.

I was in a great mood when I got
home after school.

Because we
☺ **didn't have any homework.**
And what's more, because we
☺ **made up with Paul.**

And then another **amazing** thing happened:
when I got to my room, Hannibal
had vanished.

All that remained were
a couple of gray feathers
lying on the carpet.

I ran straight to Mom, who told me that Mrs.
Lopez's daughter had picked Hannibal up.

Because Dad had
called her.

He'd told her he couldn't
correct dictations with
that critter screeching
all the time.

And he couldn't
hear the news
on TV, either.

As they carried Hannibal out,
he squawked what sounded like

Lotta is goo

Mom told me.

I went to my room and picked up the feathers.
Weirdly enough, all of a sudden I felt just a
tiny little bit sad.

I put the feathers in my keepsake box,
alongside my tiny baptism bracelet with
rubies and Grandpa's golden teeth that I
got when he died.

keepsake box

Cookies

ruby

baptism bracelet

Grandpa's golden teeth

Then I closed up the box and started getting excited for this afternoon. 🙂

For **THE WILD RABBITS** and the treehouse and Paul. **Because he really is a valuable member of our squad.**

Bernadette Bester

From my class
→ a total snob

Kevin Bester

↱ brother of

The coolest boy at school
(according to Cheyenne)

Bernadette's Gang →
The G~~lam~~ Girls
LAMB

Emma, Hannah, Maggie

always looking sternly
over her glasses

our class teacher →

Mrs. Crabbert

↳ The **Rockers**

Matthew, Finn, Tim, and Benny

Pesky brothers ↳

Jacob and Simon Petermann

Twins

Leads the school orchestra →

Mr. Yang

Polly and Mrs. Lopez

she has a bird,
named - - - - - - - - - - →